Coral
the Reef
Fairy

by Daisy Meadows

ORCHARD

The fairies must be in a dream
If they think they can be called "green".
My goblin servants are definitely greenest
And I, of course, am by far the meanest.

Seven fairies out to save the Earth?
This idea fills me with mirth!
I'm sure the world has had enough
Of fairy magic and all that stuff.

So I'm going to steal the fairies' wands
And send them into human lands.
The fairies will think all is lost
Defeated again, by me, Jack Frost!

The Green Fairies

For Maddy and Daisy Fisher,
with lots of love

Special thanks to
Sue Mongredien

ORCHARD BOOKS
338 Euston Road, London NW1 3BH
Orchard Books Australia
Level 17/207 Kent Street, Sydney, NSW 2000

A Paperback Original
First published in 2009 by Orchard Books.

A CIP catalogue record for this book is available
from the British Library.

ISBN 978 1 40830 477 8
5 7 9 10 8 6

Printed in Great Britain

The paper and board used in this paperback are natural recyclable
products made from wood grown in sustainable forests. The
manufacturing processes conform to the environmental regulations
of the country of origin.

Orchard Books is a division of Hachette Children's Books,
an Hachette UK company

www.hachette.co.uk

Contents

Magic Sparkles

Kirsty Tate beamed as she stepped onto the beach. "This looks *fun!*" she exclaimed, gazing around in excitement.

Her best friend, Rachel Walker, was close behind. "And there's so much to do," she said, her eyes bright. "Where shall we go first?"

The two girls had come with their parents to Rainspell Beach, where the local surfing group was holding a 'Save the Coral Reefs' event. As Kirsty and Rachel looked around, they could see a crowd of people dancing to the lively beat of a samba band, a line of food stalls which all smelled delicious, and an information centre surrounded by flags covered in pictures of brightly-coloured tropical fish.

"Maybe we should split up and meet back here in an hour for lunch?" Mr Walker, Rachel's dad, suggested.

"Good idea," Rachel replied. "We'll meet you at the information centre at twelve, shall we?" She slipped an arm through Kirsty's. "Come on, let's explore." The girls made their way into the crowd, enjoying the hustle and bustle of the event.

They were here on Rainspell Island for a
week's half-term holiday and so far they'd
had a very exciting few days, helping
their new fairy friends, the Green Fairies.

"There's another good reason for going
off on our own," Kirsty said, thinking
about the adventures they'd had
lately. "We might
meet another
fairy today."

Rachel grinned
and held up crossed
fingers. "Here's
hoping!" she said.

At the start of the
week, Kirsty and Rachel had magically
transported themselves to Fairyland to ask
King Oberon and Queen Titania for their
help to clean up the human world.

They had met seven fairies-in-training
who were each allocated a special
mission; when their training was complete,
they would become the 'Green Fairies',
helping to save the environment in both
the human world and Fairyland. But
before they could be given their wands
and start work, Jack Frost had appeared.
He'd declared his goblin servants were the
only truly 'green' creatures, and had
ordered them to snatch
the magic wands and
hide them in the
human world!

Rachel was peering
around expectantly,
Kirsty noticed, as if
she were hoping a fairy
would fly right up to her.

Kirsty gave her a nudge, and said in a low voice: "Remember what Queen Titania always says – there's no point looking for magic."

Rachel nodded. "I know – it'll find us," she agreed. "OK, let's go and learn about coral reefs, then."

The two friends wandered over to an information stall which had lots of colourful pictures pinned up.

As they got closer, they could see that
the pictures were of a tropical reef, with
rainbow-coloured fish swimming over
twisty coral. "Doesn't the coral look
amazing?" Kirsty said, pointing at it. "Its
shape makes it look like a weird plant."

"Well, it *is* alive,"
said a curly-haired
woman behind the
stall, overhearing her.
"Did you know
that? Coral
is a living,
breathing
organism,
covered in
limestone."

"Is it?" Rachel asked in surprise. "I
thought it was just rock."

The woman shook her head. "No," she said. "It's alive – although more and more coral is becoming damaged and dying these days."

"How does it become damaged?" Kirsty asked in interest. She remembered all the pretty pink and white coral she and Rachel had seen when they'd helped Shannon the Ocean Fairy find her stolen enchanted pearls.

"Global warming is a big problem,"
the curly-haired woman replied. "Coral
reefs can only live within a certain
temperature, but the oceans have become
warmer, which means the coral gets sick
and dies. Also, disturbances from ships and
people can damage the coral, too.
Sometimes just touching it is enough
to kill it."

Rachel and
Kirsty both felt
sad. While
they'd been
helping the
Green Fairies,
they'd learned a
lot about things like global warming,
and knew just how much damage was
being done to the planet.

They thanked the woman and wandered
further along the beach, past the samba
band and some of the food stalls. It was a
sunny day, and very warm for October. "I
love the way the sea sparkles in the light,"
Kirsty said, looking out at the rolling waves
which rushed in, foaming on the sand.

"Something over there is sparkling too,"
Rachel said, pointing to the far end of the
beach. "Look!"

The girls stared at a rock pool near
the beach's edge, where the cliffs curved
around.

Rachel was right – something in the pool appeared to be glimmering incredibly brightly, the light dancing over the surrounding rocks.

The two girls walked towards it curiously. Then, as they drew near to the rocks, Rachel let out a gasp of delight. Climbing out of the rock pool was a shiny pink crab…and there on its back, dangling a foot in the water and leaving a trail of sparkly bubbles, was a tiny, smiling fairy!

Into the Sea

"It's Coral the Reef Fairy!" Kirsty said
in excitement.

"Hello again," Coral called, waving
at them. Her shoulder-length blonde
hair was cut in a choppy style. She
wore a bright pink and orange top,
a ruffled yellow and orange skirt
and a pretty pink necklace with a
coral shape dangling from it.

Rachel and Kirsty smiled as Coral
thanked the crab and fluttered towards
them. "There's been a sighting of my
wand," she told Kirsty and Rachel. "I
was wondering
if you'd
come with
me to try
and get
it back?"
"Of
course,"
Rachel said

at once. "Where has it been seen?"

"Near one of the biggest reefs," Coral
replied. "Three goblins have been spotted
there, and one of them has my wand.
Apparently, they're not doing a very
good job of hiding."

Kirsty and Rachel exchanged glances.
That didn't
surprise them!
Jack Frost's
goblin servants
might be
sneaky, but
they weren't
exactly the
cleverest

creatures in Fairyland.

"We've got a long way to go, but I
have a little bit of magic, so I should be
able to take us all there," Coral went on.

Rachel glanced around quickly,
making sure nobody was watching them.
Luckily, the three of them were tucked
away at the far end of the beach, and
were virtually out of sight.

Coral saw Rachel looking around. "I can work my magic so it seems as if no time passes while you're with me," she assured the girls. "Nobody will notice that you've gone."

"Great," said Kirsty, feeling tingly with excitement. "Let's go!"

Coral smiled and waved her hand. A cloud of pink and white fairy dust fell over Kirsty and Rachel, and they immediately began to shrink, until they were the same size as Coral, with pretty wings on their backs!

"OK," said Coral, "now to get you into the water…"

Kirsty bit her lip as Coral waved her hand again. Into the water? Even though the sun was shining, she was quite sure the sea would be freezing! She gazed down at the water doubtfully… but then saw that two bubbles had appeared on the surface, glistening with golden sparkles.

"Take one of these each and put it over your head," Coral said. "It'll help you breathe underwater."

"Oh, we did this before when we met Shannon, Kirsty," Rachel said. "Do you remember?"

She took one of the bubbles and pulled it over her head. It looked like an old-fashioned diving helmet. Then, with a pop, the bubble disappeared.

Kirsty did the same, and then the three friends fluttered into the sea. To Kirsty's surprise, the water felt quite warm as they ducked under the waves. "Thank goodness!" she laughed. "I thought it was going to be really cold – but it feels lovely in here."

Coral grinned at the look of relief on her face. "My fairy magic will keep us all warm and dry," she said.

"Are you ready? Then off we go!"

She took Kirsty and Rachel's hands, then murmured some magical-sounding words. A second later, the three of them were being swept along at top speed through the water.

They were whizzing along so fast, Kirsty could hardly see. She could just make out blurred colours and great streams of bubbles as they were carried along in the rushing magic. It was like the fastest fairground ride she'd ever been on. "Wheeeeee!" she cried in excitement. "This is brilliant fun!"

A Funny Fish

After a few moments, Kirsty and Rachel
felt themselves slowing. The underwater
world swung into focus as they came to
a stop, and they could see once more.
Both girls looked around curiously.

The water surrounding them was a clear
aquamarine blue, and shoals of brightly
coloured fish swam in all directions. "Isn't
it beautiful?" Kirsty breathed.

"And there's the coral reef!" Rachel said, pointing in front of her. The reef stretched a long way into the distance and all three of them gazed at its knobbly structure, like a million fingers reaching up. Colourful anemones grew in its crevices, their fronds waving with the current, and all kinds of fish and other sea creatures swam through and around the reef.

The sand below them sparkled gold, and large white shells lay on the seabed.

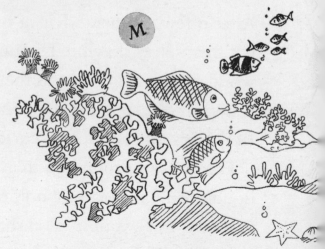

"It's like another world down here,"
Kirsty marvelled, taking it in. And then
her mouth fell open in surprise. "Look at
that fish!" she cried, pointing. "Is it really
juggling?"

They all looked at the orange and
white striped fish which
was deftly throwing
and catching tiny
white shells with
its fins.
Coral grinned.
"It's a clown
fish," she said.
"Let's go and
say hello.
He might
have seen the
goblins."

The three friends swam over to the clown fish who eyed them curiously.

"Hello, hello, hello," he said, still juggling. "What's the fastest creature underwater?"

"Hi," Coral said. "No idea. What *is* the fastest creature underwater?"

"A motor-pike!" the clown fish chuckled, dropping his shells with laughter. "Get it? A motor-*pike!*"

Kirsty and Rachel giggled. "Excuse me," Rachel said politely. "We were wondering if—?"

"Knock knock," the clown fish interrupted.

"Who's there?" chorused Kirsty, Rachel and Coral.

"Whelk," said the clown fish.

"Whelk who?"

"Welcome to the reef. Pleased to meet you!" the clown fish hooted, slapping his sides with his fins. "Get it? Whelk-ome!"

"We get it," Kirsty smiled. "I don't suppose you've seen—?"

"Why did the lobster blush?" the clown fish interrupted, tossing one of the white shells up again and balancing it on his nose.

"Listen, we really need your help," Coral put in. "We're looking for—"

"Because the sea weed!" the clown fish

shouted, spinning a somersault as he laughed at his own joke. "Please!" Rachel cried. "Can't you be serious for a moment?" The clown fish stopped laughing and stared at them, as if seeing them properly for the first time.

"Serious?" he repeated. "Oh, it's not my job to be serious," he told them. Then he thought for a moment. "Mind you," he went on, "if I *was* going to be serious, I might tell you that I'd seen some strange green creatures swimming near the reef earlier. Climbing all over it, they were, not seeming to realise that they might be damaging the coral."

"Thank you," Rachel said, relieved to have got a straight answer at last. "That's really helpful. Where were they?"

The clown fish pointed a fin. "That way," he said. Then he smiled. "I say, I say, I say…" he began.

But Coral beckoned Kirsty and Rachel away. "Sorry, we've got to go," she called to the clown fish as they swam off in the direction he'd shown them. "Thanks again! Great jokes!"

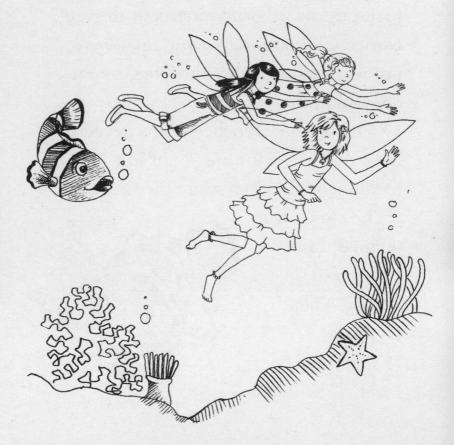

The three friends swam into the reef, with Kirsty and Rachel both marvelling at the sights around them. There were fish of every shape and colour, unusual sea plants sprouting from the sand, scuttling crabs and majestic sea turtles who raised their flippers in greeting. Then came a shout. "You're it!"

Coral's eyes grew wide. "Goblins," she hissed. "And it sounds as if they're very close by!"

Dangerous Water

Coral grabbed Kirsty and Rachel and
dragged them behind a large clump of
seaweed. She peered through its fronds,
then put her finger to her lips as she
turned back to the goblins. "The goblins
are right in front of us," she whispered.
"And you should see the way they're
jumping all over the reef. They could
cause terrible damage doing that!"

Kirsty and Rachel peeped cautiously at the three goblins. They were all wearing helmets and flippers and seemed to be playing tag around the reef, leaping from one part to another without a care. Then Rachel nudged her friends as she saw what one of the goblins was holding.

"The wand!" she hissed. "Right there!"

"The sooner I get it back, the better," Coral fumed. "What is he *doing* with it?"

The three friends stared in horror as they saw the goblin poking holes in the reef as he tried to tag another goblin with it. "Ow!" squealed a small yellow fish as the goblin accidentally jabbed at it.

"I can't bear to watch any more," Coral said. "Come on, let's try and get the wand off him."

41

She, Kirsty and Rachel swam out
from their hiding place
towards the goblins…
but before they'd
got very far, one
of the goblins
shouted a
warning cry.
"Over there!
A horrible
fairy and her
do-gooder
mates! Quick,
lads, swim!"
The goblins
immediately surged
through the water
away from Coral,
Kirsty and Rachel.

"Hurry," Coral shouted to Kirsty and Rachel. "They're getting away. After them!"

The three friends sped after the goblins, keeping a close eye on the one carrying the wand – they mustn't let him out of their sight! It was difficult, swimming fast through the reef, though; its twisty structure meant that Kirsty, Rachel and Coral had to go carefully, in order to avoid touching it, which slowed them down.

Unfortunately, the goblins had no such worries, and bashed the reef carelessly with their big flippers. It wasn't long before the speedy goblins had pulled so far ahead that Rachel, Kirsty and Coral had completely lost sight of them.

"We don't even know which direction they went," sighed Kirsty. "They could be anywhere by now!"

Rachel was about to speak when a huge shadow loomed over the three of them, blocking the sunlight and making the water feel colder and much darker. She looked up anxiously, wondering if it was a shark, or another large sea creature above, causing the shadow. But it was neither. "It's a boat," she realised, staring up at its underside.

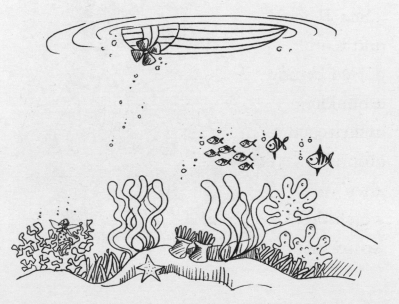

"Yes," said Coral in dismay. "And look what's just jumped off it!" She pointed at the water ahead, which was churning with great splashes and bubbles. As the bubbles cleared, Kirsty and Rachel saw a group of people who'd dived into the sea, all wearing masks and snorkels.

"Quick, hide!" Kirsty gasped. "We mustn't let them see us!"

She, Rachel and Coral darted behind a boulder and peeped around it to watch the swimmers.

Some carried special underwater
cameras and photographed the sea
creatures, gesturing excitedly to
each other.
Some wore
big flippers
– and
Coral
groaned
as she
noticed
several

people clumsily kicking the reef with them.

"Oh dear – more damage," she
said sadly. "I'm sure they're not doing
it on purpose, but they're not taking
enough care. Let's see if I can help."
She waved her hand in a pattern
and muttered some magic words.

A stream of pink-rimmed bubbles appeared near the snorkellers, surrounding their flippers and gently moving the people away from the coral reef.

"That's better," Rachel said. "Well done, Coral! Now, let's keep looking for the goblins. We've got to find them before any of the snorkellers spot them."

Kirsty nodded at once. She knew that it would be a disaster if any other humans found out about Fairyland, or its magical inhabitants. "Well, there's no sign of them here," she said, looking around, "so perhaps—"

She broke off as she spotted something even more alarming than goblins. Floating along on the surface of the water was a large collection of jellyfish, their pale pink bodies gleaming, and a mass of ribbony tentacles dangling in their wake.

"Get back!" Coral warned, grabbing Kirsty and Rachel and pulling them away as the jellyfish drifted dangerously near. "If any of us are stung, we'll be in big trouble!"

Bubble Trouble

Kirsty, Rachel and Coral swam quickly down to the bottom of the seabed to avoid the jellyfish. A shout went up from one of the snorkellers, who'd also spotted them, and the group of people went back to their boat, looking nervous.

After a minute or two, the jellyfish had passed by, and the three friends were able to set off in search of the goblins once again.

51

They plunged deeper into the reef,
looking everywhere for a glimpse of
green. Rachel had lost count of the times
she'd mistakenly thought a patch of jade
seaweed was a goblin leg when all
of a sudden she heard
voices again.

"He shoots...
and he scores!
What a goal!"

Kirsty and
Coral had
heard the
voices too, and
they all stopped
swimming to
dive behind the
reef and peer
cautiously out.

There were the goblins a small distance away – and this time they were kicking and throwing a ball of seaweed through the water.

"And look – they're using the reef as a goal!" Kirsty sighed. Coral had had enough. She swam out, furious. "You goblins are damaging the reef," she told them. "You've got to be more careful – it's a living thing, you know!"

The three goblins
stuck their
tongues out as
if they didn't
care. "We're
just having a
bit of fun," the
first one told
Coral
scornfully.

"Why don't
you keep your
fairy nose out of our
business?" the second goblin chimed in.

"Just ignore her, boys," the third goblin
said, who was carrying the wand. "There's
nothing she can do to move us away from
the reef while I've got this – and she
knows it!"

Coral gritted her teeth, and seemed on the verge of losing her temper but Rachel whispered in her ear. "Actually, you *can* move them if you want to," she reminded Coral in a low voice. "The same way you moved the snorkellers away from the reef."

Kirsty, who'd come close enough to hear too, joined in. "And maybe you can use your magic to move other things too – like your wand, out of the goblin's hand!" she suggested.

"I'll try," said Coral, "but my magic
might not be strong enough."

She took a deep breath then waved
her hands and chanted some magic
words. A stream of pink bubbles suddenly
appeared around the wand, and the
goblin who was holding it looked startled.

"Hey!" he yelled, as the bubbles dragged
him forward a little way. "Something's
pulling this wand. Help me!"

His two friends swam to him at once and grabbed hold of him, hauling him back. "Hold tight to it," one of them urged him.

"Don't worry," the goblin with the wand replied. "I'm not letting go of it – not ever!"

He clung on and after a few minutes, the bubbles popped. He jeered at Coral. "Is that the best you can do? Pathetic!" Then he kicked the seaweed ball back to the other goblins. "Let's carry on with our game."

Kirsty's shoulders slumped in disappointment. It hadn't worked. "We need another plan," she said. "And quick, before they decide to swim off again."

Rachel gazed around, hoping to find inspiration.  She shuddered as she saw that another cluster of jellyfish had appeared above them...and  then an idea popped into her head.

"I think I've got it," she said slowly, thinking it through. "What if the goblin with the wand thought it was leading him into danger? Surely *that* would be enough to make him let go of it?"

Goodbye, Goblins!

A frown creased Coral's pretty face. "What do you mean?" she asked.

"I mean, what if you could make the wand move again, but this time send it upwards, not towards us," Rachel said, the words tumbling out of her in eagerness. "If the goblin thought he was getting dragged up by the wand to those stinging jellyfish, I bet he would let go of it then!"

Coral's eyes shone. "Good thinking, Rachel!" she said.

Kirsty grinned at her friend's clever plan and then spoke in a voice loud enough for the goblins to hear. "Come on, let's leave the goblins to play their game, it's too dangerous to hang around here any more."

The goblin with the wand looked triumphant. "At last — someone who talks sense," he sneered. "Hear that, lads? Dangerous, she said. Scared silly of us goblins, clearly. And quite right too!"

Coral stared up at the jellyfish, pretending to be terrified. "Yes, those are the really dangerous kind," she said loudly to Kirsty and Rachel. "Come on, girls, we must get away quickly."

The goblins all looked up then… and their faces dropped as they spotted the jellyfish. "Oh no," one of them said fearfully. "They're not scared of us, you idiot. *That's* what they're scared of – those jellyfish!"

Kirsty, Rachel and Coral turned and swam away from the goblins, then hid behind the reef so they could keep an eye on them.

All the goblins looked worried by the jellyfish but it seemed as if none of them wanted to admit it. "I'm not scared," blustered one. "The jellyfish are right up near the surface of the water, and we're all the way down here. We'll be fine, I'm sure."

Coral winked at Kirsty and Rachel. "Let's see if he's so confident in a minute," she whispered, waving her hands and muttering some magic words.

A stream of bubbles immediately moved through the water, surrounding the wand and tugging it upwards. The goblin holding it was taken by surprise as he was dragged up with it, towards the jellyfish.

"Hey! What's happening?" he yelped, his eyes bulging in fear as he rushed through the water. "Help me, lads! Help!"

His friends grabbed his legs as he
whooshed upwards, but this time they
couldn't pull him back down. Now all
three goblins were heading straight for the
cluster of jellyfish.

"Noooooo!" they screamed.

"They're going
to get us!" wailed
the goblin with
the wand.

"Let go of
that stupid
wand,
then!"
one of
his
friends
shouted.

Rachel and Kirsty could tell by the first goblin's face that he really didn't want to let go, but as he came just centimetres away from the jellyfish tentacles, he gave a squawk of fright and threw it away. As he let go of the wand, he fell back through the water, and so did his two friends.

Down tumbled the goblins, their arms
flailing…and Coral zoomed out from her
hiding place and used her special bubble
magic to send the wand whizzing into
her hand. "Hurrah!" she cheered in
delight.

"Aarrrrgh!" the goblins shouted as,
one by one, they plunged
into a huge bed of
slimy brown
seaweed.

Kirsty and Rachel couldn't help laughing as the goblins, all tangled up, with seaweed draped over their heads and bodies, broke into furious bickering.

"I think it's time for you three to go back to Fairyland as soon as possible," chuckled Coral, and waved her wand to send them on their way with one last blast of bubble magic. The bubbles whizzed the arguing goblins into the distance, and they vanished.

"That was so funny," Kirsty giggled, and then hugged Coral.

"And how wonderful that you've got your wand back!" Coral smiled. "I know," she said. "I've got lots of work to do now, to make sure the reefs aren't damaged any further. I feel really flattered that the king and queen have trusted me with such an important job; I'm determined to do my best for them – and for the oceans!" She twirled her wand in her hand. "Thank you for helping me, girls. I should send you back to Rainspell Island now."

Rachel hugged her goodbye. "Glad we could help you," she said. "Bye, Coral."

"Bye!" called Kirsty, just as Coral waved her wand. A stream of sparkling bubbles enveloped the girls and they found themselves whirling around very fast.

A few moments later, they were back on the beach where they'd started their adventure. They were their usual sizes again, and completely dry. And, just like Coral had promised, it was as if no time had passed.

"Wow," Rachel said, smiling happily at Kirsty. "That was so exciting."

"Wasn't it amazing, being near a real coral reef?" Kirsty sighed. "I hope Coral can keep it healthy with her magic."

Rachel nodded. "We'll have to help her," she said. "We can spread the word about the problems facing the reefs so that everyone knows how to protect them, too."

"Maybe we can make some posters to put up in the surf shop and the snorkel-hire place?" Kirsty suggested. "Especially if we mention being careful with flippers around the reef. That will help get the message out, won't it?"

"Good idea," Rachel said. "And Mum does lots of work online – we can ask her about setting up a coral reef website, maybe…"

Kirsty linked an arm through Rachel's as they wandered back to the stalls. "This is turning out to be such a brilliant week," she said. "I can't wait to see what will happen tomorrow!"

**Now it's time for Rachel and Kirsty
to help...**

Lily the Rainforest Fairy

Read on for a sneak peek...

"Look, Kirsty," Rachel Walker called as
she hurried through the trees, "I think
I've found some wild onions!"

"Oh, great!" Kirsty Tate, Rachel's best
friend, ran to join her, swinging her
basket. The two girls were on a nature
walk in the forest near their holiday
cottages on Rainspell Island, where they
were spending the half-term week with
their families.

Rachel and Kirsty knelt down and
peered at the onion plants. They had
long, thin leaves and greenish-white

flowers, and in the middle of the flowers were little onion bulbs.

"The Junior Naturalist class we went to this morning was fun, wasn't it, Kirsty?" Rachel said with a smile. "I never realised there were so many things to eat growing wild on Rainspell Island. Have you got the soup recipe the teacher gave us?"

Kirsty took a leaflet labelled 'Mushroom Soup' out of her basket.

"Remember, Jo told us that we should only take as much as we need," Kirsty reminded Rachel. "Otherwise the plant won't be able to seed itself, and then it might die."

Rachel checked the recipe ingredients. Then carefully she removed some of the onion bulbs and put them in Kirsty's basket. The girls had already collected some sprigs of sweet-smelling wild thyme, and other herbs.

"Now we just have to find some mushrooms, and we can make soup for dinner tonight, with our mums' help!" Rachel jumped to her feet. "We must remember to check the booklet about mushrooms that Jo gave us, Kirsty, because we have to be sure the ones we find aren't poisonous."

"Isn't it amazing how many different plants and animals there are in the forest?" Kirsty remarked as they wandered off along the path again...

Read Lily the Rainforest Fairy to find out what adventures are in store for Kirsty and Rachel!

Meet the Green Fairies

Rachel and Kirsty must rescue the Green Fairies'
magic wands from Jack Frost, before
the environment is damaged!

www.rainbowmagicbooks.co.uk

Meet the fairies, play games
and get sneak peeks at
the latest books!

www.rainbowmagicbooks.co.uk

There's fairy fun for everyone on
our wonderful website.
You'll find great activities, competitions, stories and
fairy profiles, and also a special newsletter.

Get 30% off all Rainbow Magic books at

www.rainbowmagicbooks.co.uk

Enter the code RAINBOW at the checkout.
Offer ends 31 December 2013.

Offer valid in United Kingdom and Republic of Ireland only.

Win Rainbow Magic Goodies!

There are lots of Rainbow Magic fairies, and we want to know
which one is your favourite! Send us a picture of her and tell
us in thirty words why she is your favourite and why you like
Rainbow Magic books. Each month we will put the entries into
a draw and select one winner to receive a Rainbow Magic
Sparkly T-shirt and Goody Bag!

Send your entry on a postcard to Rainbow Magic Competition,
Orchard Books, 338 Euston Road, London NW1 3BH.
Australian readers should email: childrens.books@hachette.com.au
New Zealand readers should write to Rainbow Magic Competition,
4 Whetu Place, Mairangi Bay, Auckland NZ.
Don't forget to include your name and address.
Only one entry per child.

Good luck!

Meet the Ocean Fairies

Naughty goblins have smashed the magical conch
shell! Kirsty and Rachel must restore it
so that the oceans can have harmony again.

www.rainbowmagicbooks.co.uk